Shepherds
to the
Rescue

Written by Maria Grace Dateno, FSP
Illustrated by Paul Cunningham

Pauline
BOOKS & MEDIA
Boston

Library of Congress Cataloging-in-Publication Data

Dateno, Maria Grace.
   Shepherds to the rescue / written by Maria Grace Dateno ; illustrated by Paul Cunningham.
       p. cm. -- (Gospel time trekkers ; [#1])
   Summary: Siblings Hannah, Caleb, and Noah, aged six through ten, travel through time and space to Bethlehem, where they meet a family of shepherds who visited the Nativity thirty years before.
   ISBN-13: 978-0-8198-7251-7
   ISBN-10: 0-8198-7251-2
   [1. Space and time--Fiction. 2. Brothers and sisters--Fiction. 3. Shepherds--Fiction. 4. Jesus Christ--Nativity--Fiction. 5. Christian life--Fiction.]
   I. Cunningham, Paul, (Paul David), 1972- ill. II. Title.
   PZ7.D2598She 2013
   [Fic]--dc23

                                        2012022676

The Scripture quotations contained herein are from the *New Revised Standard Version Bible: Catholic Edition*, copyright © 1989, 1993, Division of Christian Education of the National Council of the Churches of Christ in the United States of America. Used by permission. All rights reserved.

Cover design by Mary Joseph Peterson, FSP
Cover and interior art by Paul Cunningham

"P" and PAULINE are registered trademarks of the Daughters of St. Paul.

Published by Pauline Books & Media, 50 Saint Pauls Avenue, Boston, MA 02130-3491

Printed in the U.S.A.

STTR KSEUSAHUDNHA10-231007 7251-2

www.pauline.org

Pauline Books & Media is the publishing house of the Daughters of St. Paul, an international congregation of women religious serving the Church with the communications media.

2 3 4 5 6 7 8 9   16 15 14 13

To Jennie,
my sister and writing buddy,
who helpfully pestered me
until I finished writing this series.

Contents

Chapter One

Out for a Ride

Our adventure started on a regular Tuesday afternoon. My older sister, Hannah, my little brother, Noah, and I finished our schoolwork and decided to go biking.

Hannah grabbed her bike and was off before Noah had his sneakers on.

"Come on, Noah! Hurry up!" I yelled as I got my bike and put a leg over the seat.

"Wait, Caleb!" called Noah, still tying his laces. He's only six, so he is always asking me to wait for him. I didn't want to wait because Hannah had already reached the road. I didn't want her to get too far ahead, but I slowed down a little bit for Noah.

I picked up speed once I hit the road. I pedaled standing up, trying to catch up to Hannah before she got to the top of the hill. That's where we usually go whenever we go biking. We're allowed to ride our bikes on the road because there's never any traffic. It only goes to our house and the Brownings' farm.

The trees in the woods on one side gave shade to most of the road, and I smelled the wonderful scent of honeysuckle. On the opposite side of the road was an overgrown field.

"Wait! Please wait for me!" I heard Noah yell from behind me.

Usually, whoever was the first to reach the top of the hill immediately went down the other side. It was great to coast down with the wind blowing in your face. Hannah was almost always first. So I was surprised to see her stop at the top of the hill and put a foot down. I pumped harder, meaning to whiz by her.

"Guys! Wait!" I heard Noah call again.

I pulled up next to Hannah and stopped too, waiting for Noah. We looked back and saw our little brother struggling up the hill.

Half a minute later, Noah pulled up beside us. "Okay, let's go!" he said with a big smile on his face.

All together, the three of us pedaled hard for a few feet, then, picking up speed, we sailed down the hill.

Okay, now here's where it gets weird.

Halfway down, something happened. When we talked about it afterward, we couldn't agree about what it felt like. To me, it was like we suddenly slowed down because the air got thick.

Hannah said, "No, it was like the air turned into water."

"But we didn't get wet," said Noah. "We just started moving in slow motion."

Anyway, what happened was this: we slowed down, then our bikes disappeared, and then we were running (in slow motion) down the hill, instead of riding our bikes! By the time we reached the bottom of the hill, we were in a different time and place.

But we didn't realize that yet.

Chapter Two

Where in the World?

"Look at us!" cried Hannah, which was completely unnecessary, because we were already staring at each other. The clothes we had been wearing had changed into very different clothes.

"What is this?" I asked, pulling on the tan-colored robe I was wearing. It had long sleeves and a rope tied like a belt around the waist. Noah's was the same. "It looks like a night-gown—a *girl's* nightgown."

"No it doesn't," said Hannah. "Don't look so disgusted."

I looked at what Hannah was wearing. Hers was the same color, but had decoration around the neck. Mine and Noah's didn't, so I felt a little better.

"What is it, then?" I asked.

"Well, it looks like—" Hannah started.

"Hey, what happened to the trees?" asked Noah, looking around.

"Good question," I said. "And the field there seems different."

"And where are our bikes?" asked Noah, turning around in a circle with a panicked look on his face.

We all turned and ran back up the hill, expecting to see our bikes lying by the side of the road or something. There was no sign of them. There was nothing but hills, dirt, and small bushes as far as we could see.

"Something happened to the road, too," said Noah.

It was true. There was no pavement. It was just hardened dirt.

We stood at the top of the hill, looking at each other.

"I wonder how this happened," I said. "I've never heard of anything like it."

"Never mind *how* it happened! We need to undo it," said Hannah. "We need to figure out how to find our house."

I could tell she was worried. Hannah is almost eleven and acts like she's responsible for us—which means she thinks she gets to decide what we do.

"Are we lost?" asked Noah.

"We can't be," I said. "It's impossible to get lost so quickly. Hannah, we don't have to be home until dinnertime. Let's walk further down the road and see what's going on."

"Yeah," said Noah.

"No, guys, we need to go home and tell Mom and Dad what happened," said Hannah.

Noah and I rolled our eyes at each other, but we followed Hannah back the way we had just come, minus our bikes.

We walked and walked. Soon there wasn't even a road to follow. The land was rocky, with some small bushes and grass and weeds that were pretty dried out. After I got used to the robe-thing I was wearing, I kind of liked it. It hung down to about my knees, but it was very loose, so it was easy to walk in it.

"Okay, Hannah, let's stop for a minute," I said, after we had been walking for what seemed like an hour. "We should have been there by now."

"And I'm thirsty," said Noah.

"Well, we didn't bring anything to drink," said Hannah.

"I'm hungry, too," said Noah.

"I had a bag of trail mix in my pocket," I said, "but . . ."

We all felt the sides of our robes—there were no pockets.

"I think we just have to keep going," said Hannah. "We have to come to our house eventually."

We walked some more and then Hannah gave in. As we sat down to rest, Noah opened his mouth to complain again. But suddenly he looked up and tilted his head to one side.

"Hey, guys, can you hear that?" he asked, smiling.

"What?" I asked. "I don't hear anything."

We all stopped and listened. Soon we could all hear what Noah heard—it was music, coming from somewhere nearby.

Chapter Three

Shepherd Boy

We jumped up and started walking toward where the sound seemed to be coming from.

"Hey, guys, look at that!" said Noah. He was pointing across the field, which was covered with some dry grass and a few little bushes. "What are those?"

We looked and saw groups of white things on the side of a small hill in the distance. Some of them were moving around.

"I think they're sheep!" I said.

"Okay, now I know for sure that we're lost," said Hannah, "because the Brownings don't have sheep. Neither do any of our other neighbors."

"And look!" Noah pointed to the left of where the sheep were, and we saw a person sitting on a rock near the sheep. As we got closer, we could see that it was a boy, and that he had his back to us.

"Oh, yay!" I said. "Maybe he has some water he can share with us."

"It would be really nice if he had a cell phone, too, and a few extra energy bars," said Hannah.

"Hello!" I called when we got close enough.

The boy turned around. He was holding some kind of musical instrument that looked like two small flutes stuck together. He looked a little older than Hannah. When he stood up, I could see he was taller than Hannah. I was glad to see he was wearing a robe a lot like mine. He also had a thing like a bandanna tied around his curly hair.

"Greetings," he said. "My name is Benjamin. Welcome!"

"Hi, I'm Caleb," I said. "This is Noah."

"And I'm Hannah. We've been walking for a long time and we're lost. Do you have a cell phone we could use?"

"A what?" Benjamin asked.

"And do you know where we can get some water?" asked Noah.

"I have water," said Benjamin, holding out some kind of soft canteen—a funny bag-shaped container.

Hannah took it and swished it. I could hear that it wasn't full. "Is this all you have?" she asked.

He nodded. I was surprised he had just handed it to her.

"Can we each take just a little?" she asked.

Benjamin smiled. "Yes, please. You are welcome to share it among you. I was soon going to move the flock over toward the well. We can go now and you will have as much water as you need. And I will refill my vessel there."

"That's very nice of you," said Hannah as she opened the stopper of the container and handed it to Noah. "Not everyone would be so generous."

Benjamin looked a little confused. "Of course I share my water with a stranger who asks me."

Noah gave me the water and I took a few gulps. That made me feel better, except that now I was hungry.

"When we get to the well, we can rest longer and have something to eat," said Benjamin as he put his flute-thing in his bag, which looked a little like a homemade duffle bag.

"If you have some trail mix or an energy bar to spare, we could eat that as we go," I said hopefully.

Benjamin looked confused.

"I do not know what those things are," he said. "But I don't think I have any."

"That's all right," said Hannah. "We can wait."

Benjamin began calling his sheep. "Jumper! Thorny! Bent-Ear!"

I laughed out loud.

"Your sheep have funny names!" said Noah.

"Yes," agreed Benjamin. "But each name is very appropriate, let me assure you."

"Two-Spot! Nose-Spot! Trip!" he called.

As each sheep responded to its name, I realized he was right. The sheep were mostly white (well, a dirty white), but Nose-Spot had a funny black splotch next to its nose. Two-Spot had black spots on either side of its tail.

Finally Benjamin got them all moving. The four of us talked as we walked along.

"Why is that one called Thorny?" asked Noah.

"When she was a lamb, I rescued her from a thorn bush," said Benjamin, smiling at this sheep.

"What about Trip? Did you get that one on a trip?" Noah asked.

"No, he is always tripping over rocks!" said Benjamin, laughing.

We continued walking slowly, with the sheep following.

"When did you come here?" asked Benjamin. "I can tell you are foreigners. Your hair looks like no one else's I have ever seen."

I looked at Noah's hair, which was very much like mine—short, straight, and sand-colored. Hannah's was pulled up in a pony tail, a darker brown, but also straight. It was nothing like Benjamin's dark brown, curly hair, which was a little long and wild-looking. His light brown skin was darker than ours would be even at the end of summer.

"Well, we just arrived," said Hannah. "We've been walking for a long time."

"Where are you traveling to, and where did you come from?" Benjamin asked.

"We're trying to get back to where we came from," said Hannah. "But—"

"We don't actually know where we are," I interrupted.

"That village you can barely see over there is Bethlehem," said Benjamin.

"Bethlehem?" asked Noah. "Like in the song?"

"Song?" asked Benjamin.

"O – lit - tle – town – of – Beth - le - hem –" sang Noah.

Benjamin looked so confused that Noah stopped.

"So, that's Bethlehem?" asked Hannah. "Do you live there?"

"Yes, but now that I help my father with the flock, we spend a lot of time out in the fields," answered Benjamin. "We have already done the second shearing, so the third day from to-day, we leave for the higher land where we'll stay for the next few months, while it's hot."

"Where is your father?" I asked. I didn't really understand what he was talking about.

"He will meet me at the sheepfold with the rest of the flock. You are welcome to come with me," said Benjamin. "Do not worry. Bethlehem is a very nice place, and my father is the head shepherd. He will help you find where you need to go."

Chapter Four

Benjamin Shares

We eventually got to the well. It wasn't what I was expecting. There was no round brick wall with a little roof over it, like you always see in pictures. It was basically just rocks around a hole in the ground. And there were other flat stones nearby that had been hollowed out in the middle. They turned out to be for holding water for the sheep to drink.

I was interested to see Benjamin take something out of the bag he carried over his shoulder. He unfolded what looked like a leather bucket and let it down into the well.

The water was nice and cool, and we all drank our fill.

"Can we eat now?" asked Noah.

"First I must get water for my sheep!" said Benjamin, frowning at Noah.

"Let me get the water for the sheep," I said. "You can start getting the food out, okay?" I wanted to try that collapsible bucket.

"Thank you, Caleb!" said Benjamin.

I took the bucket and began hauling up water. It took a lot longer than I thought it would because the sheep were thirsty and the bucket didn't hold very much—otherwise it would be too hard to pull up.

As I was hauling the water, the other three sat down by the well. Benjamin opened the bag he had carried over his shoulder.

"We don't want to eat all your food, Benjamin," said Hannah.

"You will not eat all of it because I am going to eat some, too!" said Benjamin with a big smile. "It will not be enough to fill us up, but at least we will not suffer the hunger so much."

Benjamin took out something wrapped in a

cloth. I was curious what kind of food it would be. There was bread, some fruit that I think was apricots, and two other things I didn't recognize. They turned out to be cheese (that looked like it would taste yucky, but didn't), and dried fish (that did taste a little yucky, but I ate it anyway).

Benjamin divided it all out, and we ate quickly. Noah wouldn't eat his fish, so Hannah ate his and gave him a little of her bread.

"What's that hanging from your belt?" asked Noah.

I had noticed it, too. It looked like leather, braided into a long string. There was a wider part in the middle—sort of like a pocket—and it was thinner on the two ends.

"This is my new slingshot," said Benjamin, smiling proudly. "My grandfather made it for me. I have been practicing. I am very good with it now. I am sure I could hit any wolf or jackal that comes near my sheep."

"Let's see," I said.

Benjamin picked up a small stone, then dropped it and picked up another one. He held the two ends of the slingshot in his hand and put the stone in the wide part in the middle. He twirled it around in the air. When he let go of one side, the stone went flinging through the air. It hit a large rock some distance away.

"Wow, that's good!" said Noah. "Were you trying to hit that rock?"

"Of course," said Benjamin. "Now I will hit that rock over there, by the little bush."

I watched closely as Benjamin twirled the slingshot over his head and directed the stone at the rock. Sure enough, it hit the center and bounced off.

"Hey, could I try?" I asked.

"Yes, you are welcome to," said Benjamin.

It looked pretty easy, so I took the slingshot and the stone he handed me. I had a little trouble getting the stone to stay in the pouch part. But after it had fallen out a couple times, I got the hang of it and started twirling the slingshot over my head.

I let go and tried to aim the stone toward the rock that Benjamin had hit, but it went sideways and landed near a sheep. It was Nose-

Spot, and he jumped and trotted away, making "baaaaa" sounds.

"Hey!" said Benjamin. "What are you doing?" He looked really angry.

"I'm sorry!" I said quickly. "I didn't mean for it to go that way. It didn't hit him, though."

"You must be careful," said Benjamin, still looking not happy. "The slingshot is to use against wild animals. It is to protect my sheep, not to hurt them or even scare them."

"Sorry," I said again. "I didn't mean to scare them." I handed the slingshot back to Benjamin.

Chapter Five

A Place to Stay

"We should get going soon," said Benjamin. "We still have a ways to go."

"Are we going into the town?" Hannah asked after Benjamin got the sheep moving.

"No, the sheepfolds are around on the other side of Bethlehem. We will walk close to the village, but it is much easier to take the sheep around than through," said Benjamin.

He was right—it was quite a long walk.

Benjamin walked ahead of the sheep and they followed. Noah walked next to Benjamin and asked him questions about the sheep and the flute he had been playing, which Benjamin called his "pipes."

Hannah walked next to me.

"I guess we just have to go with Benjamin and talk to his father. Maybe he can help us," said Hannah.

"Yeah, and if he doesn't have a cell phone either, he could tell us where the nearest phone is," I said.

"It just seems funny: Benjamin didn't say he didn't *have* a cell phone. He didn't know what we were talking about at all," Hannah said.

"Yeah, that is kind of weird," I said.

The sheepfold wasn't what I was expecting at all. I guess I was thinking of white fences, like on a farm. But this was made of stone walls in a square shape. There was an opening on one corner, and we headed that way.

I was hoping that it was almost time for dinner because I was starving.

"Abba!" called Benjamin as we got closer. He ran ahead and went through the opening.

"What did he say?" Noah asked me.

I shrugged and followed Benjamin into the sheepfold.

Benjamin was there hugging a man who looked so much like him I knew right away it was his father.

"Welcome," he said, turning to us. "My name is Simon. We are very happy to have you here."

We told him our names, and he said that most of the others were not back with their flocks yet.

"Only Eldad and I are here, but we will prepare the evening meal because you must all be very hungry," said Simon.

"*I am*!" said Noah. I was kind of surprised that he hadn't been complaining. I mean, he knew there wasn't anything to eat, but that didn't stop him from complaining in the car when Mom was driving us somewhere and we didn't have any snacks.

"Benjamin, what did you call your dad?" Noah asked as we went to sit in an area of the sheepfold that had a roof over it. There was a small fire there.

"My what?" asked Benjamin.

"Your father," I said. "What did you call him?"

"'Abba,' of course. What do you call your father?" asked Benjamin, looking confused.

Simon came over and introduced his father, Eldad. Eldad had a curly beard that was black with some white mixed in.

"So, you're Benjamin's *grand*father!" Noah said, smiling at Eldad, who sat down next to us.

"Yes, that would be right," he said. "I am very proud of my grandson, who is doing such a good job with the flock." He smiled at Benjamin, who smiled back. Eldad had crinkles by his eyes when he smiled.

"Tomorrow we must speak of your plans," said Simon. "Benjamin told me that you are lost. And you do not have parents with you, so we must decide where you will go."

I was hoping we could stay with them, but I thought it would be rude to ask.

"Could we stay with you?" asked Noah.

"Noah!" said Hannah, embarrassed.

"You can stay with us until the third day, Noah," said Simon kindly, "but then we must leave for the highlands and you cannot come with us."

"They can come with me tomorrow, Abba," said Benjamin. "I need to bring the sheep past the crossroads in order to find grazing for them. It will be good to have company."

"Very well. But when we leave, they will have to stay in Bethlehem. Perhaps they can stay with your mother," Simon said.

After we ate our delicious hot meal we were ready to go to bed.

We certainly must have been tired to be able to fall asleep on the ground. They only had blankets—not even any sleeping bags. I didn't think I'd be able to get comfortable, but I slept all the way through the night.

Chapter Six

The Accident

When I woke up, it took a few seconds for me to remember where I was. Then I jumped up to see what everyone was doing.

One of the shepherds was making breakfast—some kind of pancake-things cooked on a flat stone in the fire. I ate mine so fast I barely noticed what they tasted like. I couldn't wait to bring the sheep out to graze.

It was great fun to go with Benjamin and help him watch his sheep, get water from the well, and talk about everything!

Late in the afternoon, Hannah came up next to me as we walked with the sheep.

"Caleb," she said in a low voice, "we need to figure out how to get home."

"Oh, yeah. We forgot to ask about where the nearest phone is. But, Hannah, this is fun!" I said.

"Mom and Dad are going to be worried!" Hannah said.

"Well, we don't know how we got here, and we don't have any money to get a plane to fly home, so what can we do?" I asked.

"Caleb, I don't think we could take a plane home even if we had the money," said Hannah. The sound in her voice made me look at her—she was worried.

"Why do you say that?" I asked.

"Well, it started with the clothes. And then Benjamin's bucket and slingshot and the well. They're so . . ." she stopped, looking like she was searching for the right word.

"Do you mean they're so old-fashioned-looking?" I asked. It was true. Everything Benjamin had seemed old-fashioned and homemade.

"I mean they all look like something from a long time ago," said Hannah. "Like, well, from the time of the Bible."

"The Bible?" I was surprised, but . . . it made sense.

"Yes, don't you see? These robes—I think they called them tunics. Don't they look just like the clothes in the movies from the time of the Bible?" she asked.

"Yeah, like in the story of Moses," I said.

"Or from the time of Jesus, or some time after Jesus, but still a long time ago," she said.

"*That* would explain why Benjamin doesn't know what a cell phone is!" I said.

"Or an energy bar," said Hannah, smiling.

"Hey, Benjamin!" I said and hurried to catch up to where he was walking with Noah.

I caught up to Benjamin and walked next to him.

"Hey, Benjamin, I know someone who was born in Bethlehem. I wonder if you know him."

"Who is it?" asked Benjamin.

"His name is Jesus. He's . . . um . . . a great teacher," I said.

"Oh! I have heard of him!" said Benjamin, smiling. "My grandfather has told me the story of his birth many times. Maybe he will tell the story tonight."

"Okay, but when—" I started to ask, but at that moment Noah let out a yell.

"Aaaaaahhh!"

We ran over to him and found that he had fallen.

"What happened, Noah?" asked Hannah as she helped him up.

"I just stepped up onto that rock," said Noah, crying. "It rolled and I fell off."

Noah had twisted his ankle, and he couldn't walk on it. Benjamin carried Noah back to the well (we had already set out toward the sheepfold) and had him put his foot in the bucket filled with cold water from the well. Benjamin emptied it several times to refill it with cold water. Then he wrapped Noah's ankle with a cloth he had in his bag and tied it tightly, so Noah could walk on it. We found him a stick as we walked along, and that helped, but we were going pretty slowly.

As the sun began to set, I noticed that Benjamin started looking around a lot more.

"What's the matter, Benjamin?" I asked.

"Well, I'm not usually this far from the sheepfolds at this time of day," Benjamin answered. "The wild animals come out at dusk, and I'm afraid they might come for my sheep."

"Can we make a torch or something to scare them away?" asked Hannah.

"I could kindle a fire, but we would have to stop and find a good piece of wood and take time to light it. I don't want to slow down or stop now. And my sheep will not want to either. They want to get to their sheepfold and settle in for the night," Benjamin said.

"We can handle wild animals, right?" I asked. "You have your slingshot, and I can throw stones. I have pretty good aim, just not with a slingshot."

"That sounds good, Caleb," said Benjamin. "I'm glad you are willing to help fight the wolves or jackals if they come."

I was definitely willing. I was almost looking forward to it. At least I was until suddenly I heard a terrible howling sound from over to our left.

Chapter Seven

Howls in the Night

"Benjamin!" I yelped as I ran closer to him. "What's that?"

The sheep were also moving closer to Benjamin. They all started *baaaaa-ing* nervously.

"That's a wolf. Let's hope it's alone. At least it's over there and not in between the town and us," Benjamin said.

"What should we do?" asked Hannah. "Should we keep going?"

"Yes! Come on. I'll carry Noah for a while," said Benjamin. "More wolves will gather now that they've heard this one howling."

We set off walking much more quickly,

with Benjamin carrying Noah piggyback, and the sheep following. They were going much more quickly, too.

Benjamin kept looking back nervously.

"Is the wolf following us?" asked Noah.

"I am looking back to make sure the sheep are following us. If they lag too far behind, the wolf will come and pick them off, one by one. I wish I could walk in the back, but they need someone to follow now, or they will not keep together," said Benjamin.

Then Benjamin looked at me and I was afraid of what he was going to say.

"Here," he said, handing me the long stick he was carrying. "You go walk behind the sheep."

"O-okay," I said, feeling the sweat trickling down my forehead. "What do I do with this?"

"Use it to hit the sheep in the back, to make them keep going," he said.

"Hit them?" I asked. I was surprised he would tell me to do that when he was so angry before that I only threw a pebble near them.

"Yes! Hit them and if they don't move, hit them hard. It's for their own good. Otherwise they'll get eaten by the wolf!" Benjamin said.

I moved to the back and started poking the sheep with the stick. They didn't need me to do much, since they wanted more than anything to get to their sheepfold as soon as possible.

"Hannah, do you think you can carry Noah?" Benjamin asked. "If the wolf comes close, I will need to use my slingshot."

"I can walk now," said Noah. "I think my ankle is a little better."

We kept going as fast as we could, but soon we heard the howling sound again. The sheep all started *baaa-ing* again, and some of them started wandering to the side or stopping in their tracks, instead of going forward. I started poking and then hitting them hard, especially when another howling sound came, and this time, from the right.

"Oh! They're on both sides now!" said Hannah.

"Yes," said Benjamin, "but we're almost

there. See the hillside up ahead? The sheep-folds are on the other side."

Just then the howling broke out worse, on all sides at once. Benjamin starting twirling his slingshot. I saw his face as he looked out toward the wolves. He looked very determined and brave. I didn't feel brave at all. I was trying to poke the sheep to make them stay in a group and keep moving, but they were getting more and more scared.

Then I saw the wolves getting closer. Hannah screamed. I saw her bend down and grab a rock and throw it at the wolves. I couldn't stop to throw rocks because I was still helping keep the sheep together. Noah was crying, but he also started throwing rocks. Benjamin seemed to be hitting a few of the wolves because once in a while I'd hear a kind of yelp.

Then suddenly Benjamin started yelling, "Abba! Abba! Abba, help!" We were very near the rocky hill.

I saw a wolf running toward Benjamin, and then I got knocked over by some crazy sheep and didn't see what happened until suddenly there were other people—grownups—around us. There were torches and lots of yelling, and they chased the wolves off.

Soon the four of us and Benjamin's sheep were in the sheepfold. Benjamin grabbed his stick from me and went around tapping the sheep on their backs. He seemed to be counting them.

"Oh, Abba!" he said to his father. "One is missing!" And he burst into tears!

"No, son," Simon said. "Look, over by the gate. There is one more."

"Oh, Trip! There you are!" said Benjamin. He ran over and bent down to hug his sheep. "I thought you had been eaten by wolves!"

"Now, Benjamin," said his father, "tell me what delayed you. We were worried."

"It was my fault!" said Noah. "I'm sorry!"

"Noah twisted his ankle, Abba," said Benjamin. "We took some time to bring down the swelling so he could walk, but he could not walk very fast. Then the wolves came!"

"Come and eat, and tell us your story," said Eldad, who was standing nearby.

Chapter Eight

A Story Retold

We had supper and told the whole story of the wolves. Benjamin's father and grandfather told us we had been very brave and did a good job taking care of the sheep.

"Now you need to sleep," said Simon.

"Oh, Abba," said Benjamin, "I cannot sleep yet. Please, may Grandfather tell us a story?"

"What story should I tell you?" asked Eldad, smiling his crinkly smile. "You have heard all my stories many times already."

"Tell the story of the angels' message. Noah and Caleb and Hannah have not heard it," said Benjamin.

Eldad smiled. "Ah, that would be good. I will tell you the story of the birth of Jesus."

I was thinking that I had heard the story of the birth of Jesus many times already, every Christmas time. I would rather have heard a different story that I had never heard before, but luckily I didn't say anything.

"It was thirty years ago," Eldad began, "during the cold time of the year. We were not far from here, and we were using a sheepfold—a larger one—that is now broken down and not used."

"Wait!" said Hannah, sitting up straight. "Did you say thirty years ago?"

"Yes, that would be right, about thirty years ago," said Eldad. He looked a little bit annoyed that she had interrupted, but I understood immediately why she had burst out like that. Thirty years ago!

"So that means Jesus is thirty years old now?" asked Hannah.

"Yes, he is now thirty, but I will tell you of the night he was born," said Eldad, trying to get back to his story.

Hannah looked at me and I could only smile at her. This meant that not only were we in Bible times, but we also now knew that we were in the time of Jesus!

Eldad continued: "The fire had burned down to nothing, and I was playing my pipes softly. Your father, Benjamin, was still in his mother's care, but your uncle Judah was with me. He was a little younger than you are now. The other shepherds were sleeping under the roof, but Judah was sleeping under the stars because it was a clear night, and he did not want to leave one of the lambs that had lost its mother."

"He was sleeping with the lamb?" asked Noah. His eyes were big and round, and I could tell he was really getting into the story. Eldad smiled. He didn't seem to mind *his* interrupting.

"Yes, he felt sorry for it. He wanted to keep it company, and keep it warm," continued Eldad. "I was the only one awake. It was so peaceful and beautiful. I stopped playing my pipes and looked up at the stars, as I had done so many times. Their beauty never ceases to amaze me. I praised God who had created such beauty.

"At that moment, as I was looking up, I saw a bright light, which quickly came closer. I was terrified and knew not what it could be. It looked as if one of the stars had come loose from the sky and was falling down on me.

"I jumped to my feet and yelled in alarm. All the other shepherds woke and came over to me. We stared at the light as it slowly settled across from us on the top of the wall. Then we could see that it was an angelic being.

"'Do not fear!' the angel said. I think we were all still afraid, but we listened as the angel continued, 'I bring you good news of great joy that will be for all people!'

"We looked at each other, and I could see in the faces of my fellow shepherds the fear and wonder and awe that I felt. Who were we that this being should come to us? The light shining from the angel made the whole sheepfold as bright as the dawn.

"The angel continued, 'Today in the city of

David, a Savior has been born for you, who is Christ the Lord.'

"Do you know what the angel meant by the 'City of David'?" asked Eldad, looking at the three of us.

"That's Bethlehem!" said Noah with much excitement.

"Yes, Bethlehem is right," said Eldad. "We knew he was saying that the long-awaited Savior had been born in our town. We understood this, but we could not believe it. How could such a thing happen to us?

"'And this will be a sign for you—you will find the baby wrapped in swaddling clothes and lying in a manger,' the angel said. We looked at each other. 'Lying in a manger?' *Why would a baby be in a manger*? I thought. But we did not dare ask this heavenly being anything. Even if we had wanted to, it soon became impossible. At that moment, the sky became as bright as noonday, with a multitude of angels filling the sky above the sheepfold. They were all singing something so beautiful that I have tried ever after to play it on my pipes, but it was not music of earth. The heavenly host sang, 'Glory to God in the highest, and on earth peace on those with whom he is pleased.'"

"Were they flying in the air?" asked Noah.

"Yes," said Eldad, smiling his crinkly smile. "They were all in the air above us. The music was so beautiful, I thought we were in heaven. Then, as suddenly as they had come, the angels were gone. We stood for many minutes, in shock, looking up at the beautiful stars."

Chapter Nine

The End of the Story

"Then what happened?" I asked. It was like I had never heard the story before. Somehow, listening to someone who had been there made it sound new.

"Then little Judah came running over to me. 'Abba!' he said. 'We must go now! We must go to Bethlehem and see the baby!'

"We all agreed that we must respond to the angel's message by going to be a witness to the good news he had given us. We talked about who should stay with the sheep, but no one wanted to be left behind!

"'We cannot leave our sheep here alone,' I said. 'If no one will stay behind, we must bring them with us.'"

"I can imagine you were worried about how hard it would be to get those sheep moving!" said Benjamin, laughing.

"Yes, we were afraid it would be impossible, or else take all night," said Eldad. "'The baby will be grown by the time we move all these flocks to Bethlehem!' grumbled one of my fellow shepherds.

"But that did not happen," continued Eldad. "It was a bigger sheepfold than this, and full of many more sheep. But each shepherd took a turn making his special call, and all the sheep got up and walked out, as if it were morning and they were eager to go graze in the hills! We walked ahead and the sheep followed."

"How did you find baby Jesus?" asked Noah.

"The angel had said the Savior would be a baby lying in a manger," Eldad said. "The stables and barns were all located on the outskirts of the city, and mostly on the eastern side. So we headed that way.

"We were still a ways from the city when suddenly we knew exactly which way to go. There was a bright light all around a small stable just ahead. It was the kind of stable made partly in a cave. We went toward it and looked inside."

"Grandfather, you did not tell them what you did with the sheep," said Benjamin.

"You are right," said Eldad. "I forgot to say that as we got nearer, the sheep just stopped in their tracks. Some of them lay down to sleep right there, and some were nibbling on the little bit of grass and the bushes in that place. This was another amazing thing that happened that night. We left them there with only one dog to guard them, and all of us shepherds—about eight of us—went up to the stable."

"Oh! And then you saw the baby, and his mother, Mary? And Saint Joseph?" asked Noah, completely wrapped up in the story.

"Eh? You know their names? Yes, the mother was there. As we looked in, she was swaddling the child, and then she laid him down in the manger, which was full of hay. We could see her husband over with the animals. He was getting feed for the donkey. We watched until they were both there by the manger, just looking down at the baby," said Eldad.

"What? You didn't go in?" asked Hannah in surprise.

"Yes, we went in," he answered, "but first we just looked in, making no noise. It was so beautiful that we did not want to interrupt. But then Judah, who was climbing on a rock to try to see better, slipped and fell. He let out a cry, and immediately the father came over to the entrance and looked out at us."

"Was he surprised to see a flock of shepherds outside the door?" I asked.

Eldad roared with laughter. "A flock of shepherds! Oh, you are right—we were like a little flock of shepherds at the door. He looked quite surprised, but I spoke up and said, 'Sir, we did not want to bother you, but an angel came to tell us about the infant Savior here, so we knew we must come to see him.'

"And Joseph looked even more surprised. 'An angel told you? What did he tell you?' he asked. So, we recounted the whole story. In the meantime, Judah crept into the stable and over to the mother and baby. We finished telling our tale, and Joseph invited us closer. Judah was already sitting next to the mother, looking down on the baby and touching his little cheek."

"And did Judah play his drum as a gift for baby Jesus?" asked Noah.

"What?" asked Eldad. "You ask such strange questions. He had no drum. But you are right that he gave him a gift, though I don't know how you knew.

"Judah went and found the little motherless lamb that he had been caring for. He gave it to the family of the Savior. It was a gift from all of us, since our sheep are all we have, and we love them as our most valuable possessions.

"I did not know it that night, but I also received a gift. From that time, even though nothing changed in my life, everything changed. I worked as a shepherd the same as before. But now I knew that God was close to me, watching me. He had known exactly where I was and had sent word to me of the coming of the Savior."

Eldad stopped talking, and we all sat there thinking. I was thinking that I had never pictured the story of the birth of Jesus so well. Just spending some time with shepherds helped me to really imagine what it was like.

"That was beautiful, Eldad," said Hannah. "Thank you so much."

Benjamin looked very proud of his family's story. "Grandfather, you did not tell them about what Uncle Judah is doing now."

"Well, that is something that is bitter-sweet," said Eldad.

"What does 'bittersweet' mean?" asked a puzzeled Noah.

"It means it's something both happy and sad," Eldad said. "You see, Judah has now stopped being a shepherd so he could follow Jesus. He is one of his disciples and travels with him all over Judea and Galilee."

"Oh!" I said. "That is wonderful! Do you know where he is right now?" I asked.

"During the last festival in Jerusalem, we were able to see Judah. It seemed they could be traveling back to Galilee, so I imagine he is somewhere in one of those towns. The teacher Jesus travels a lot."

Chapter Ten

The End of the *Other* Story

When the story was over, I was suddenly so tired. Noah fell asleep right where he sat.

The last thing I heard before falling asleep was Eldad telling Benjamin, "Rest well. We have a big day ahead of us."

When I woke up the next morning I remembered what Eldad had said and wondered what exciting thing we would be doing!

"Good morning, Caleb!" said Benjamin. "I am glad you are awake. I must bring you to Bethlehem so you can stay with my mother and sister and little brother. Today we must leave with the sheep for the highlands."

"What?" I asked. "I didn't know that was today! Didn't you say you were leaving in three days? It's only been two!"

Well, it turned out he had said that they were leaving on "the third day." They counted one day as the "first" (the day we met Benjamin), then the next day as the "second" (the day Noah twisted his ankle), and the next day as the "third" (which was today).

Noah was disappointed, too. I could tell. But Hannah hurried him through breakfast so we could walk with Benjamin to Bethlehem. Noah was not happy about being hurried, but no matter how much we dragged our feet, soon it was time to go.

We said goodbye to Simon and Eldad. They were busy organizing supplies.

As we walked, I wondered if I would see Benjamin again. I swallowed the lump in my throat.

"Are you happy to go with your father and grandfather, Benjamin?" I asked as we got near the town. "Don't you miss your mother and sister and little brother?"

Benjamin looked confused at my question. "You do ask funny questions," he said. "Of course I am happy to go with my father. That is what a boy should do. I am learning to be a good shepherd, as my father and grandfather have been. I love my mother, but now that I am old enough, I must go and work. For shepherds, that means that at this time of year, we have to be away from the town, so the sheep can eat. It is hard work to take care of sheep, but when it is time to shear them, we will have lots of fine wool. Then my mother and sister will work hard to clean the wool and prepare it for selling to the merchants. Did I answer your question?"

"Yes, thank you," I said. "It was great to meet you and see how you take care of your sheep. I think you will be a very good shepherd."

"Thank you. I hope so. But you know, I never asked you what your father does," said Benjamin.

"He makes wooden toys and furniture," said Noah, "and sells them online."

"What?" said Benjamin, with that confused look on his face. I needed to explain to Noah that Benjamin wouldn't be able to understand these kinds of twenty-first century things.

"He's a carpenter," I said.

"Oh, look!" said Benjamin. "Do you see those stables? The second one is where Jesus was born. My grandfather always points it out to me when we pass."

"What?" I exclaimed. "Oh, we have to go see it!"

"Please just look quickly and then come to my house. It is at the end of this street. The very last one," Benjamin said.

"We'll be right there!" said Hannah, as the three of us ran toward the stable.

The stable Benjamin had pointed to looked a lot like the one next to it. We would never have known which one it was if Benjamin hadn't told us.

We hurried to the door and pushed it open. There was a donkey standing in the corner. Next to it was the manger. It was just a box made of rough wood. There was straw on the floor.

As we stepped inside, the air became thick, and we were moving in slow motion. Immediately I realized what was happening. *No!* I thought. *I don't want to go back yet!*

And then we were standing beside the dirt road, with our bikes on the ground next to us. We stood there just looking at each other for a few seconds. We had our old clothes back on, and the trees were where they had always been.

I took a deep breath. "Was that real? Were we really there?"

"Well, it couldn't have been a dream if we were all there, right?" asked Hannah.

"It wasn't a dream!" said Noah. "It was real!"

"Wow. That's all I can say," said Hannah. "Wow."

Chapter Eleven

What Just Happened?

"Benjamin is going to wonder what happened to us!" said Noah.

"Never mind Benjamin. What do we tell Mom and Dad?" I asked, suddenly realizing that we would need to explain where we'd been for two nights. "For sure they've been worried sick."

"What can we tell them?" asked Hannah. "They'll never believe us. The whole thing is impossible. I mean, if you and Noah came and told me that this had happened to you, I'd be sure you were making it up."

"But we can't lie!" said Noah.

"Nooo," said Hannah slowly. "Well, let's just see how it goes. We don't need to blurt out the whole story right away," she said, looking at Noah.

"I won't do that," said Noah.

We got our bikes and walked them up the hill. It seemed about the same time of day as when we had ridden down the hill two days before. We got on our bikes once the hill wasn't so steep, and slowly rode back to the house.

We left our bikes leaning up against the workshop, as usual. I peeked in the window and was surprised that the light wasn't on. I tried the door and it was locked.

"That's funny," I said. "Usually Dad would be working out here now, wouldn't he?"

"Yeah, he's always here at this time of the afternoon," said Hannah. "Maybe he's out with a search party or something!" she added, looking worried.

"He works every afternoon except on Sunday," said Noah.

"Sunday?" I asked. "It was Tuesday when

we left! It can't have been five days!" I looked at Hannah to see what she thought.

"It definitely wasn't five days. It was two nights," she said. "Let's go inside and see if anyone's around."

We went to the side door and opened it. Mom was in the kitchen, at the counter, stirring something.

"Hi, guys," she said, glancing over at us. "I decided to make some apple cake. Who wants to lick the bowl?"

We just stood there, staring. I was trying to figure out why Mom wasn't acting surprised or happy or relieved or anything. She was acting as if we had just been out riding our bikes for a bit.

"So, how's it going, Mom?" I asked.

"How's what going?" she asked as she started pouring the batter into a cake pan. "The cake? I could make this kind of cake in my sleep," she said.

"Where's Dad?" I asked. "Why isn't he in the workshop?"

"He just left to go into town. He asked if

you all wanted to come, but I said you'd just
gone out bike riding."

We still just stood there, staring at her. Why
wasn't she asking us where we'd been?

"What's with you guys?" she asked, looking over at us. "You're acting like you're guilty
or something. What have you been up to?"

Noah had a big smile on his face. He was about to blurt out the whole story. I could tell.

"Mom! We went to Bethlehem!" Noah burst out. Hannah and I looked at each other.

"Bethlehem?" asked Mom. "That sounds like fun."

"Yes! We met a shepherd boy named Benjamin and helped him with his sheep and got chased by wolves and made it to the sheepfold." Noah was all excited, but I could tell Mom wasn't taking him seriously.

"Wow, Noah. Sounds like you had quite an adventure."

Mom thought that we had been pretending. Luckily, Noah didn't seem to get it.

"Mom, I want to get out our nativity set! Benjamin's grandfather is one of the shepherds who were there. And the angel—lots of angels—came and told them about baby Jesus."

"Well, Noah, the nativity set is put away with the Christmas decorations," said Mom.

"I know, but I want to look at it! Please?"

"Well, all right," said Mom. "After I get this cake in the oven, we can go find the box."

Hannah and I went off to her room to talk, while Noah and Mom went to the basement to get the nativity set out of the boxes of Christmas decorations.

"So," I said, sitting in the chair at Hannah's desk. "Mom and Dad didn't even notice we were gone."

Hannah plopped down on her pink flowered bedspread.

"Yeah," said Hannah. "It seems like it. Although I can't figure out how."

"What time did we go out bike riding?" I asked, looking at the alarm clock by her bed.

"I don't know. I think it was around two o'clock," she answered.

"It's 2:19 now," I said.

"And it must be the same day, since they didn't even notice we were missing," she said.

We just looked at each other. I was thinking about walking with Benjamin and listening to his grandfather as we sat around the fire. It all seemed so real. How did it take less than half an hour for all of it to happen?

"I think," said Hannah slowly, "that maybe it's like you read in books. Kids go to another world and years go by, but when they come back to our world, only a few minutes have passed."

"But Hannah, we didn't go into another world. Jesus was born in Bethlehem in our world. We traveled to another time, not another world," I said.

"True," she said. "But I think it still applies. Anyway, the whole thing is impossible. There's no way to travel back in time, just like there's no way to travel to other worlds. It can only happen in books! It's not something we can figure out."

"I guess . . ." I said. I mean, I wanted to be able to figure it out, but I had to agree, it was just impossible.

We heard Noah with Mom in the living room. They were getting the nativity set out, unwrapping all the pieces. We listened in the hallway.

"Here's Mary," said Mom.

"And here's another shepherd!" said Noah.

"And the last one is the third wise man," said Mom.

"There aren't enough shepherds," said Noah. "There were a lot more than two."

"I think you're right, Noah," said Mom. "There were probably several of them, watching their sheep as they grazed in the grass."

"No, Mom," Noah said. "They weren't grazing. They were sleeping—it was night time."

"Oh, you're right. Sheep sleep at night, just like people."

"Yeah, and the shepherds had to get them all up and bring them to find baby Jesus," said Noah.

"I never thought of that," Mom said.

Chapter Twelve

The Good Shepherd

After our Bethlehem adventure, something in me felt different.

I understood what Eldad meant when he said that nothing in his life had changed, but everything had changed. I did the same stuff I usually did each day, but on Sunday, when we went to church for Mass, I realized what was different.

Father Joe read the part from the Bible where Jesus talks about being the Good Shepherd. I got my dad to help me find it in the Bible when we got home. Here it is:

"I am the good shepherd. The good shepherd lays down his life for the sheep. The hired hand, who is not the shepherd and does not own the sheep, sees the wolf coming and leaves the sheep and runs away—and the wolf snatches them and scatters them. The hired hand runs away because a hired hand does not care for the sheep. I am the good shepherd. I know my own and my own know me, just as the Father knows me and I know the Father. And I lay down my life for the sheep. I have other sheep that do not belong to this fold. I must bring them also, and they will listen to my voice. So there will be one flock, one shepherd" (John 10:11–16).

It was neat to hear how Jesus talked about sheep and shepherds!

"Now, we know that Jesus was a carpenter," Father Joe said in the homily. "So why does he say here, 'I am the good shepherd'?"

Good question! I thought.

"He is not saying that he was actually a shepherd," Father Joe continued, "but that our relationship to him can be compared to sheep and shepherds.

"For example, he talks about how a shepherd takes care of his sheep. When a wolf attacks, a shepherd wouldn't run away and leave the poor sheep behind to get eaten."

That was so true! I turned to look at Noah and he was smiling at me. I knew he was remembering how Benjamin stayed with his sheep when the wolves came. And how he had burst into tears when he thought one of them was missing.

"He would defend his sheep and keep them safe," Father was saying, "even if it meant risking his life. So, the same thing is true for Jesus. He doesn't abandon us when we need help. And the worst danger for us is sin, because when we sin we are going away from God. So Jesus came to earth to bring us back to God, to bring us safely to heaven. And he was willing to do that even though it meant dying on the cross."

It was so neat to think about Jesus as my shepherd. I had never thought about him like that. And so I did something I don't think I had ever done before. I talked to Jesus just to talk to him, not to ask for something or because I had a problem.

Jesus, I prayed, *I feel like I kind of know you better now, after being with a shepherd and seeing how he took care of his sheep. He was so brave when the wolves were around us. I want to be like that. I want to be brave in doing what I'm supposed to be doing. I don't know when I will have something hard to do, but when I do, I know I can be brave because you are with me to keep me safe.*

Well, I did ask for one thing.

Please, Jesus, please, please, I want to really know you. Please let me see you!

Where Is It in the Bible?

Like Caleb, you have probably heard the story of the birth of Jesus many times. The part about the angel coming to the shepherds can only be found in the Gospel according to Luke. Here it is. As you read it, imagine the story as Eldad told it:

In that region there were shepherds living in the fields, keeping watch over their flock by night. Then an angel of the Lord stood before them, and the glory of the Lord shone around them, and they were terrified. But the angel said to them, "Do not be afraid; for see—I am bringing you good news of great joy for all the people: to you is born this day in the city of

David a Savior, who is the Messiah, the Lord. This will be a sign for you: you will find a child wrapped in bands of cloth and lying in a manger." And suddenly there was with the angel a multitude of the heavenly host, praising God and saying,

> *"Glory to God in the highest heaven,*
> *and on earth peace among those whom*
>   *he favors!"*

When the angels had left them and gone into heaven, the shepherds said to one another, "Let us go now to Bethlehem and see this thing that has taken place, which the Lord has made known to us." So they went with haste and found Mary and Joseph, and the child lying in the manger. When they saw this, they made known what had been told them about this child; and all who heard it were amazed at what the shepherds told them. But Mary treasured all these words and pondered them in her heart. The shepherds returned, glorifying and praising God for all they had heard and seen, as it had been told them (Luke 2:8–20).

Written by Maria Grace Dateno, FSP
Illustrated by Paul Cunningham

Three ordinary kids, six extraordinary adventures, one incredible quest!

Join Caleb, Hannah, and Noah as they're whisked away to the time of Jesus and find themselves immersed in some of the most amazing Bible stories of all!

Coming soon! Mystery of the Missing Jars (#4), Courageous Quest (#5), and Discovery at Dawn (#6)

Who are the Daughters of St. Paul?

We are Catholic sisters. Our mission is to be like Saint Paul and tell everyone about Jesus! There are so many ways for people to communicate with each other. We want to use all of them so everyone will know how much God loves us. We do this by printing books (you're holding one!), making radio shows, singing, helping people at our bookstores, using the internet, and in many other ways.

Visit our Web site at www.pauline.org

BOOKS & MEDIA

The Daughters of St. Paul operate book and media centers at the following addresses. Visit, call or write the one nearest you today, or find us at www.pauline.org

CALIFORNIA
3908 Sepulveda Blvd, Culver City, CA 90230   310-397-8676
935 Brewster Avenue, Redwood City, CA 94063   650-369-4230
5945 Balboa Avenue, San Diego, CA 92111   858-565-9181

FLORIDA
145 S.W. 107th Avenue, Miami, FL 33174   305-559-6715

HAWAII
1143 Bishop Street, Honolulu, HI 96813   808-521-2731

Neighbor Islands call: 866-521-2731

ILLINOIS
172 North Michigan Avenue, Chicago, IL 60601   312-346-4228

LOUISIANA
4403 Veterans Memorial Blvd, Metairie, LA 70006   504-887-7631

MASSACHUSETTS
885 Providence Hwy, Dedham, MA 02026   781-326-5385

MISSOURI
9804 Watson Road, St. Louis, MO 63126   314-965-3512

NEW YORK
64 West 38th Street, New York, NY 10018   212-754-1110

PENNSYLVANIA
Philadelphia—relocating   215-676-9494

SOUTH CAROLINA
243 King Street, Charleston, SC 29401   843-577-0175

VIRGINIA
1025 King Street, Alexandria, VA 22314   703-549-3806

CANADA
3022 Dufferin Street, Toronto, ON M6B 3T5   416-781-9131